# Sherlockian Ruminations

# from a Stormy Petrel

## Brenda Rossini

ePub ISBN  978-1-78092-708-4
PDF ISBN  978-1-78092-709-1
Paperback 978-1-78705-055-6

Published in the UK by MX Publishing
335 Princess Park Manor, Royal Drive,
London, N11 3GX

www.mxpublishing.com

Cover compiled  by  Brian Belanger

# Contents

Christian Sacraments and

"The Adventure of the Devil's Foot"

*Christianisacramentumrubor* -- There are a welter of sacramental alternatives to this puzzle and the devil is in the details: "Each is suggestive, and together they are almost conclusive." Arthur Conan Doyle, educated in a Jesuit school, was attracted to the mystical, spiritual, and sacramental. He dabbled perversely and symbolically with these not-so-subtle motifs in *The Devil's Foot*: "Neither of us is prepared to admit diabolical intrusions into the affairs of men..." Yet so it is, and the other-worldly excursion brings murder to a peaceful, card-playing community.

**Baptism** begins Christian life, cleansing the new life of its original sin, and becomes the gateway towards receipts of the rest of the sacraments. Devil's advocate Dr. Sterndale, who lived "beyond the law" and Christianity in Africa, returned to civilization with a devil's ritual, the *Radix pedisdiaboli,* which uncorked the whole diabolical intrigue. But he brought it along only as a curiosity. He was but a pilgrim. It was the perfidious Mortimer Tregennis who found a use for it in Cornwall.

A baptism by fire takes place at the Tregennis house, nearby a stone cross which does not save the acolytes. The Tregennis' are consumed by an airborne devil's root, burning like incense, from which effects one is dead and the others driven mad. The baptism accoutrements include fire, guttered candles, ashes, and a lamp, presumably containing oil, but not from the vicarage's holy font where Holmes acquired his portion.

There are no water immersions with *Radix pedisdiaboli* but water symbolism abounds:

---Mounts Bay, to which waters, like Lourdes, Holmes has gone for his health; it will be a life-affirming respite,

5

and one where guilt and crime will be identified and confronted.

--- Holmes' clumsy stumbling over water pots-- "So absorbed was he in his thoughts, I remember, that he stumbled over the watering-pot, upset its contents, and deluged both our feet and the garden path". Alas, foot washing is not a sacrament but a Christian ritual amongst disciples. The wetting of the feet is a creative deviation from Christian dogma. In baptism, water is poured on the head. Here, Holmes' "baptism" occurs when the contents of the water pots are spilled and poured upon his feet.

---When Dr. Sterndale stood outside the Tregennis house, a morose figure looking in at Brenda, the rain may appear as baptismal, though the reader must assume that Sterndale had been baptized.

***Holy Orders:*** The word "priest" is the Latin derivation of the Greek "presbyteros" meaning an "elder." Priests through the ages were authoritarian hierarchies over a credulous public, whether the Druids of neolithic man, Chaldeans, a colonial explorer, or African medicine men who used devil's root to seal ordinations.

Vicar Roundhay was elderly and "intrusive," enlisting unworthies as his priests to solve the devil's crimes. To invest with Holy Orders, there is a laying of the hands. When Roundhay was with Tregennis in Holmes' room, Watson observed a "twitching of his thin hands." Tregennis and Roundhay shared a "common emotion." Tregennis dressed formally for the occasion, entrusted to solve a crime which he committed. But he had his own agenda; he was a rogue priest with the devil's root as his "special Providence."

Another priest in the thicket was Sterndale. He lived an ascetic, monk-like existence "amid his books and maps...(in) an absolutely lonely life...almost like an anchorite." The vicar was in his confidence; they knew and respected one another. When Sterndale went off to Africa, the vicar wired him because he required his services.

**Holy Eucharist:** At mass, Christians partake of a wafer and wine from a chalice-- the verisimilitude of body and blood from a crucifixion in the Middle East; they receive spiritual power in the transfer and life is revealed. The devil's root, half-human and half-goat, brought by Sterndale "under extraordinary circumstances in the Ubangi country," was ingested as a powder in an ordeal ceremony--madness or death was the fate. The root would kill on contact.

Holmes tested his hypothesis of the crime. He bought a lamp like Tregennis'. He lit it and filled it with oil. He says the oil is from the vicarage---it's holy. Watson serves as godparent. Once lit, the poisonous devil's root ash is expelled into the air and they are both overcome.

Another Eucharistic example was the family Tregennis' final meal, but in their case, the dining occasion was a precursor to the ending of life and not an affirmation of life. The three siblings were eating with the killer in their midst and not their savior. It has evocations of the Last Supper.

**Confirmation:** The believer and a sponsor reflect on their eucharistic decision and commitment. For this "ceremony," Holmes conducted a life-threatening experiment with the devil's root....until there is "no longer doubt." The depth of Watson's commitment is evident:

    "I dashed from my chair, threw my arms round

Holmes, and together we lurched through the door and in instant afterwards had thrown ourselves down upon the grass plot and were lying side by side, conscious only of the glorious sunshine which was bursting its way through the hellish cloud of terror which had girt us in. Slowly it rose from our souls like the mists from a landscape, until peace and reason had returned, and we were sitting upon the grass, wiping our clammy foreheads, and looking with apprehension at each other to mark the last traces of   that   terrific   experience which we had undergone."

Mortimer Tregennis perverts the affirmation of a spiritual life when, in order to secure for himself the family financial legacy, he hellishly dooms the physical lives of his siblings.

*Matrimony*--Dr. Sterndale and his wife could not divorce even though she'd left him. Thus, the sacrament of eternal union brought pain to Sterndale and Brenda Tregennis, the woman he loved; the devil's root brought death.

*Penance/Confession*--to   be   saved   from   eternal consequences, the sinner receives spiritual counsel and leaves consoled after confession. Sterndale is summoned by Holmes and confesses.   Absolution is administered simultaneously as per Christian doctrine. Instead of referring him to the authorities, Holmes sends Sterndale off to "bury" himself in Central Africa as penance and a form of future last rites.

Mortimer Tregennis was confronted by Sterndale about the devil's foot and about a similar fate then awaiting him. Sterndale described Tregennis as a "wretch" and "paralyzed." Was it for fear and was he repentant in his last five minutes on earth?

***Extreme Unction***---Last rites were administered by Sterndale for Mortimer Tregennis, the criminal in the first tragedy but a victim in the second. Sterndale walked to Tregennis', carrying with him gravel in preparation for the ritual dirt to be thrown on a grave...dust to dust, ashes to ashes. He threw it up at the window where Tregennis was to die. He forced Mortimer to sit beside the lamp into which he poured devil's foot powder and watched from outside the window with a pistol. Sterndale was not seeking to heal with the sacrament but to enact his revenge.

Mortimer Tregennis disposed of his family at a last supper; how perverse was his role as their judge and executioner.

Was Conan Doyle sacrilegious? Or devil-may-care with ancient dogmas and certainties? Perhaps. More likely, he was a keen weaver of tall tales: Sterndale's gravel? *Devil's Foot* was published in 1910. Two years prior, Charles Dawson reported that a skull fragment was found in a Piltdown gravel pit. Doyle commemorated for posterity that elemental gravel. Likewise his unholy adventure with the sacraments was a fitting accompaniment to his greater enterprise--spiritualism.

Death Comes to Pemberley's Debt

to Boscombe Valley

*Cooee! Death Comes to Pemberley*involves a murder imposed within the woods of Pemberley by mystery author P.D. James, both eminent and grise (age 92).

James' plot flits between Jane Austen's *Pride and Prejudice, Persuasion, Emma,* and *Sense and Sensibility,* but what is not acknowledged is that the pastoral murder most foul is drawn *in toto* from Conan Doyle's *Boscombe Valley Mystery*...the details of a woodland hit that was first deduced by Sherlock Holmes.

The characters are there for the finding, culled from Jane Austen's stories. The mystery arcade, however, is from *Boscombe*. Holmes set out the murder scene for Watson, point by point-- easy enough to follow for an author's blood-stained right hand in search of a plot.

**SUSPECTS:**

The suspect in *Pemberley*?*Pride and Prejudice* villain-- Wickham the *casanova di* prepubescent females. He was also a close friend of the victim Col. Denny, he comes forth from the wooded site, blood-stained and drunk.

In *Boscombe*?the prodigal son, James, age 18 is accused of murdering his father Charles McCarthy. James came running up to the lodge almost immediately after Patience Moran had heard him quarreling with his father. He was in a shocked state, and his right hand and sleeve were stained with fresh blood.

**THE SCENE**

an isolated, wooded copse

**WITNESSES** (there were none at either murder scene):

In *Boscombe*, William Crowder, a gameskeeper, saw Charles going towards the woods, and soon after, he saw James going down that same path, carrying his gun. Patience, the 14- year-old, was picking flowers. She said there appeared to be a violent quarrel between father and son McCarthy. She said she saw James raise his hand as if to strike his father.

In *Pemberley*, George Pratt, the coachman, said that after Wickham, Lydia, and Capt. Denny were through carousing at a pub, Pratt drove them in the chaise towards Pemberley. Then, there was a heated quarrel between these two friends:

"halfway into the woodland Captain Denny knocked to stop the chaise," got out and said: 'I'm finished with it and with you.' He then ran off into the woodland  Wickham went running after him."

About 15 minutes passed and then Lydia and Pratt heard the shots. No one was in the  copse but Wickham and Denny. Denny was shot and killed.

Mr. Darcy unfolds the Pemberley mystery as mannered, gentleman detective. He retraces the steps of the chaise and its passengers and walks through the "remote" and "tree-guarded" wood. It was nighttime, and they could see little but what their lanterns shone upon."

## ACTUAL ASSAILANT IN THE WOODPILE

In both *Pemberley* and *Boscombe*, two ailing, seemingly incapacitated individuals holding grudges.

## THE BODY

McCarthy was "stretched out upon the grass"..."the head had been beaten in by repeated blows of some heavy and blunt weapon." It was initially surmised that the injuries looked to be the kind inflicted by the butt end of James' gun.

## CONFESSIONS

In *Pemberley*, Wickham weeps over Capt. Denny's body, which is on its back, his right eye caked with blood, his left, glazed, fixed unseeing on the distant moon. Wickham was keeling over him, his hands bloody, his own face a spattered mask and confessed responsibility for his best friend's death.

## THE ACTUAL WEAPON

a slab of stone hidden in the moss

## BOTH STORIES COMMENT ON THE VICTORIAN CRIMINAL JUSTICE SYSTEM

Conan Doyle consistently spoke with disfavor about the criminal justice system.

An inquest was held in Boscombe on the next day, Tues. and James was bound over for "wilfull murder." The murder occurred on Monday.

What made Boscombe Valley an object of desire? Was it the obscurity of the story? Here then was a fresh turn of an old plot, but let's acknowledge the gift(s) of Holmes.

Jack the Ripper as *shanda*

With Charles Nicholls' re-shuffling of Jack the Ripper suspects in *Traces Remain*, one becomes perplexed by the Ripper graffiti in 1888 which announced "The Juwes are the men That Will not be Blamed for nothing"--the translation of which might be, *you cannot just continue to blame us (the Jews)*! Or, in the alternative, *if Jews must be blamed for something, here is something that will really cause a Ripple.*

The evidentiary details of the Ripper crimes were that five prostitutes, alcoholic and destitute, were murdered and their corpses mutilated with a bladed instrument. These unsolved murders occurred in the early hours, between Aug. 31 to Nov. 9, 1888, in the untypical quiet of London's overcrowded immigrant district of Whitechapel where Jews and Irish swelled the squalid ranks (no fog-lapped windowpanes). These women died while working, on the street, except for the last one who died in her lodgings.

South African historian Charles van Onselen identified one "Joe" the Ripper, aka Joe Fox/ Joe Silver as the sexually-motivated perpetrator. Fox lived in South Africa, having traveled to that British protectorate from New York and London in the late 1890s. He may have made a brief stop in Whitechapel in the 1890s but there was no recorded connection or transit in the relevant time period of the murders...1888.

According to Hartley Nathanin *Who Was Jack the Ripper,* "The authorities and upper classes assumed that the perpetrator must be a foreigner or a low-class savage." Numerous Ripperologists also profiled a suspect from the upper classes--one who wandered through this immigrant community unrecognized. Nicholl observed correctly that identification of the Ripper as Jewish may have been anti-Semitic scapegoating, but that it was more likely a possibility than not.

A Jack the Ripper suspect was reported to have worn astrakhan. Symbolically, in literature and in journalistic reporting, "swarthy" men wore astrakhan, and so we find this garb in Arthur Conan Doyle, T.S. Eliot, and in Evelyn Waugh, the latter two being particularly disposed towards ethnic disparagement. The Ripper was reported to have worn a hat, and in one sighting, it was purportedly described as a "deerstalker." Jewish men always wore hats; a traditional habit. British workmen were not so obliged.

Van Onselen's Joe Fox was a pornography entrepreneur (new on the Victorian horizon), brothel-keeper and criminal habitué…an immigrant trying to make a large living and unable to do so legitimately. Most of theJewish suspects were excluded by dates, alibis, and other negations, but one persisted, and it was not Joe Fox. It was Aaron Kosminski. He featured in the early police investigations upon witness identifications. Robert House persuasively placed him as the killer in *Jack the Ripper and the Case for Scotland Yard's Prime Suspect*.

Aaron emigrated with his family from Russo-Poland about 1882, at age 17. In those little towns, Jews were familiar with blood libel accusations—knife-slaughter and mutilation of gentile children for Jewish rituals. Aaron would also have observed the common ritual slaughter of chickens for the weekly shabbos table.Living alone in Whitechapel, behind his family in a back-room shelter, Aaron was variously reported as an infrequent hairdresser, tailor, and as a laborer in Butcher's Row.

All was not without serendipity in Whitechapel. In 1880, author Charles Fox published a celebrated version of

*Sweeney Todd, the Demon Barber of Fleet Street.* Sweeney Todd was dedicated to slitting the throats of the upper class, and, inspired by utilitarian theories, converted the victims to tasty meat pies for the poor. He didn't really exist but in Aaron Kosminski's time, Sweeney and his bloody habits was performed to enthusiastic audiences again and again. In 1888, the year of the Ripper murders, Benjamin Farjeon, himself an immigrant resident of Whitechapel, published his version, *Devlin the Barber.* The legend played on in musical ditties, penny dreadfuls and in serializations as shilling "shockers."

The murders:
Mary Ann (Polly) Nichols, discovered 3:40 a.m. Fri. Aug. 31.
Annie Chapman, last heard at 5:30 a.m., Sat. morning Sept. 8.
Two on one day: Liz Stride 12:45 a.m. and, about 1:45 a.m., Catherine Eddowes, early morning Sun. Sept. 30.
Mary Jane Kelly, last seen or heard in her lodgings, 2:30 a.m., Fri. Nov. 9.

Two of the murders fell proximate to the Jewish High Holy Days which in 1888 were: Thurs. Sept. 6 -- Rosh Hashanah 1;
Fri. Sept. 7-- Rosh Hashanah 2; Sat. Sept. 15, Yom Kippur.

Three died before or after the weekend shabbos (Fri. sundown through Sat. sundown).

None of the prostitutes was Jewish though there were Jewish prostitutes. Sadie was not always a lady. According to van Onselen, as well as Conan Doyle's colleague and fellow spiritualist William T. Stead in his anti-white slavery campaigning, Jewish pimps controlled East End brothels and transported their women to American haunts. Joe Fox may have found his career in this manner.

Jewish prostitutes awaited their customers indoors. The Ripper sought vulnerable women who wouldn't recognize him and wouldn't have a pimp in the shadows. It may be that Whitechapel streets were lighter in night traffic in a community observing, fasting, or breaking the fast within the home.

One of the victims was killed in the vicinity of a church where the women often stood. Catherine Eddowes was picked up around the corner from Rabbi Hermann Adler's Great Synagogue and her customer was observed by two Jewish congregants.

All the victims were killed within a mile of the Spitalfields market and slaughterhouses. Annie Chapman may have met her customer in Spitalfields. The Ripper killed the women at their street assignations, except for one.

With the victim subdued, he cut her throat, from left to right. He would have been blood-soaked but workers in their leather aprons were commonplace. They came through Whitechapel towards home, or to the public sinks, or the cesspools. The graffiti about "the Juwes" was inscribed after Eddowes' murder, above a passage leading to Aaron Kosminski's lodgings.

Then, the murders stopped. There may be more victims on this list, but the opinions about them remain mixed because of divergences in the manner of death or method. Ripperologist, Martin Fido, in The Crimes, Detection and Death of Jack the Ripper, searched through asylum records to explain the cessation of the murders. Aaron Kosminski had been certified a lunatic and committed permanently to a London asylum in 1891. His family may have sheltered him. A witness who may in fact have identified him, perhaps in the asylum before he was permanently committed, refused to testify against a fellow Jew and see him hanged.

Nicholl was left unpersuaded by Patricia Cornwell's accusation of the artist Walter Sickert in *Portrait of a Killer*. In his Ripper study, Hartley Nathan devoted a chapter to "My Favorites" none of whom is Jewish or Cornwell's Walter Sickert.

# Ruddy Annotations to the

## *Red-Headed League*

"How in the name of good fortune" did Arthur Conan Doyle specifically choose red heads and then gather them within the nomenclature of a league? There was rhyme and reason behind Doyle's tricks, and unmistakably saucy.

No drafts of *The Adventure of the Red-Headed League* are available to Sherlockian researchers, and it is unknown whether any exist. Perhaps one is hidden in the "w" section of an 1890 Encyclopedia Britannica. The title of the story is as eccentric as the rest of the *Red Headed League's* circumstances: the obese, untidy, dim-witted pomposity of a former pawnbroker sitting in Sherlock Holmes' rooms, red-headed applicants crowding the city street, the longhand transcription of an Encyclopedia as a job assignment. The bank robbery may have come courtesy of heist man Adam Worth (see Ben Macintyre's excellent book, *The Napoleon of Crime: The Life and Times of Adam Worth, Master Thief*). So did Conan Doyle lift these particularities from events simmering in the London of 1890 and 1891.

I propose a few possibilities, concededly in the realm of coincidence, but persuasive nonetheless. Let us recall that Holmes himself remarked on the tug of coincidence which applied during his investigative stream of observation, deduction and analysis: "Amid the action and reaction of so dense a swarm of humanity, every possible combination of events may be expected to take place, and many a little problem will be presented which may be striking and bizarre..." *The Adventure of the Blue Carbuncle*.
The connections in the *Red Headed League* are to the Salvation Army and to the suffragettes, both unnerving annoyances to the public and to Conan Doyle.

*The Red Headed League* was published in August 1891 (though Watson recorded an entry of 1890). William Booth

(1829-1912) founded the Salvation Army in 1865. He was a resident of Tunbridge Wells and of London, both places familiar to Conan Doyle. Before he embarked on his evangelizing Christian career, William Booth had been a pawnbroker's assistant. How inapposite! Booth left pawnbroking because, having witnessed the plight of the poor and the debt-ridden, he believed that Christian salvation would ameliorate the inequalities. A character in *the Red-Headed League* was named after a Marxist in London's Socialist League, William Morris--an agitator for workers and their wages (in *RED*, the pay was £4 pounds a week; England's workers were generally paid about £60 a year.)

Relations between the Salvation Army and Conan Doyle were prickly. The Army and Booth were actively opposed to spiritualism. The evangelical message was adherence to the message of Christ and not devotion to fairies and angels. They also preached strict temperance. They marched, invaded saloons, proselytized, and baptized. They collected money in villages and towns and established international missions. Their distinctive kettles, in which they collected donations, were symbolically red: red for the wounds of Jesus Christ. In 1890, Booth published *InDarkest England and the Way Out,* about the horrors of life in England's slums.

Booth was a public figure and became the scourge of a hostile and suspicious press. He and his soldiers were assailed as charlatans. Cartoons questioned what he would do with all the money he collected, and he was accused of hoarding donations.

Booth was also mocked for "elevation of women to man's status," for he gathered women into the various leagues of his Army...the League of Love, the League of Mercy, or the

Missionary Tea League. He allowed them to preach publicly, traditionally a male province, and the women hectored loudly against gambling and drink. Booth's wife and daughters became militant suffragettes and Tunbridge Wells was their campaign center.

Ezekiah Hopkins founded a League in his search for red heads (through the efforts of John Clay):

> "As far as I can make out, the League was founded by an American millionaire, Ezekiah Hopkins, who was very peculiar in his ways. He was himself red- headed, and he had a great sympathy for all red-headed men; so when he died it was found that he had left his enormous fortune in the hands of trustees, with instructions to apply the interest to *the providing of easy berths to men whose hair is of that colour. From all I hear it is splendid pay and very little to do.'"* (italics, ed.)

Booth's Salvation Army became an international concern and a family foundation, with places on the board for each of his children. Most compelling of Willliam Booth's children was Evangeline Booth (1865-1950). In 1887, at age 21, she graduated from hawking the Army's "War Cry" paper to become an officer of a corps in Marylebone where there was strong opposition to the Salvation Army.

Holmes lived on Baker St. in Marylebone, a middle class neighborhood near the slums and the former gallows. The Army was unwelcome in this polite society primarily because many of them had come from the class of the wretched, the poor, former alcoholics, morphine addicts, and prostitutes.

Then, in 1890, at a time when women were becoming energized in their struggle for civil rights and the right to vote, Evangeline was named General of her father's Army. She spoke before many social reform Leagues: women's leagues, prison reform leagues, leagues for political education, and temperance leagues.

In 1889, Evangeline was among the founders of the Women's Franchise League in England which would evolve into a satellite of the League of Women Voters in America. England's women publicized their struggle for the vote by cycling throughout the country...some, we can presume, were even solitary cyclists in the countryside.

Women and their campaigns, as well as their cycling predispositions, began pushing cricket out of the media spotlight. Conan Doyle, a member of the Allahakbarries of upstanding batsmen and also the Marylebone Cricket Club, was an excellent and enthusiastic cricketer. He was nominally supportive of the women's cause, but only just so. Conan Doyle agreed in the granting of civil rights to women and reform of the divorce laws, but he believed women were to conduct themselves in restrained manner. Suffragettes often chained themselves to railings and set fire to mailbox contents, or in Conan Doyle's case, despoiled his mail with lye. At least one cricket team wore the suffragette colors in support--Green, White, and Violet (Give Women the Vote). It has been suggested that Sherlock's name was derived from two of Conan Doyle's fellow ball players.

Years later, in 1955, Sheldon Reynolds (of Andrea Reynolds' and the case of the contested Arthur Conan Doyle estate fame) produced "The Case of the Careless Suffragette," with Ronald Howard starring as Sherlock

Holmes, in a magnificently puerile script based on Conan Doyle's latter day opinion that suffragettes were responsible for "monkey tricks," such as the burning down of a cricket field in Tunbridge Wells. The film was about a zealous but ingenuous suffragette who acquired a green croquet ball shaped like a bomb. She intended only to draw attention to the suffragette cause. As fate would have it, the ball, switched by an unworthy heir, exploded and killed a member of Parliament.

Suffragettes in the movie---except for the star--were homely oddities. Yet, in real-life Evangeline Booth was a pistol of a personality. Descriptions of Evangeline were that she was red-haired, red-hot, and righteous! That red hair and Evangeline's public prominence was catnip to Conan Doyle's pen when writing the *Red-Headed League.*

Evangeline's activities were in the daily papers-- the campaigning, organizing, demanding, and facing riotous crowds. As the applicants in the *Red-Headed League* crowded the streets of Saxe Coburg Square in hopes of employment, so too in 1890 did the suffragettes gather and protest, at the Great Suffragette Demonstration in London.

Jabez Wilson was as "tenacious as a lobster" in committing the entries of the Encyclopedia Britannica to paper, in longhand, though he got only as far as the "a's." Why this book? Why the longhand?

Shorthand was in vogue. Shorthand enthusiasts contacted one another in Victorian-era magazines, including the *Strand,* which published the Sherlock Holmes' stories. Women could now enter the workforce as typists (*Case of Identity*) and as stenographers for which skills they trained in women's schools. Strong, healthy men wouldn't need to engage in these secretarial activities where now a woman's delicate hand would be more amenable to the venue and the lower wages.

In these revolutionary times, developing technologies allowed women to earn incomes, yet barred them from the rights accorded men, whether in wages, inheritance, or marriage. In1890, the 9th edition of the *Encyclopedia Britannica* was published and it acknowledged the women's cause. It was the first of its editions with a chapter under "W" devoted to "Women, Law Relating To." This edition would have been available to Jabez Wilson though it would have taken him months to reach the penultimate volume.

Thus did the *Red Headed League*, Sherlock Holmes, and Conan Doyle unwittingly acknowledge the women's movement with that pawky touch of red. It was an accidental nod, since Conan Doyle was striving to keep it at 1895, but the serrated side plot would live to see another day.

Sherlock Holmes: the Jewish Connection--Who was that Hebrew Rabbi?

It is next-to-impossible, and just as improbable, that either Sherlock Holmes or Arthur Conan Doyle would have contemplated Rabbi Akiva of ancient Israel as the "Hebrew Rabbi" in *Scandal in Bohemia*.

No less collapsible was the fanciful idea that New York Rabbi Samuel Adler and his reformist inclinations were contemplated by Holmes in his index, or that Irene Adler was a New York converso. A late Sherlockian, Ruth Berman, identified Rabbi Hermann Adler as the "Hebrew rabbi" (reference to Ms. Berman's conclusions supplement Les Klinger's comments to *Scandal in Bohemia*, at p.17, of The New Annotated Sherlock Holmes (N.Y.; W.W. Norton & Co. 2005).

In ACD's world, the sun rises only upon the British Empire (which was still some years before the vivisection in The Guns of August). The "Hebrew rabbi" can be attributable only to the British family Adler.

> *"This is indeed a mystery," I remarked. "What do you imagine that it means?" "I have no data yet. It is a capital mistake to theorize before one has data. Insensibly one begins to twist facts to suit theories, instead of theories to suit facts...."*

### Supplemental Twistings:

*Did Holmes study Hebraic texts?* ---- Neither Rabbi Akiva's (circa 40 C.E. – 140 C.E.) texts, nor the mishnah (debates) nor talmud--the written codes of oral Jewish traditions-- were translated into English in the late 1800s. Whatever did arrive in Europe, following the fiery immolations of the Romans, came from manuscripts taken with the diaspora or from Egypt. Rabbinical students in Europe read the texts in the original...Aramaic *cum* biblicalHebrew. The talmud was not available in the vernacular until AdinSteinsaltz began publishing segments of his monumental text, *The Essential Talmud*, beginning in the 1980s, in modern Hebrew. In 1989, English translations appeared. Thus was the talmud opened to international and lay study. Where do we read that Holmes was familiar with biblical Hebrew or Aramaic?

Holmes' Biblical proclivities are most Christian, deriving from Arthur Conan Doyle's Christian bible and as representative of a Christian nation. When Holmes discovers, accuses, or pardons a transgressor, he speaks from a Christian perspective. *"I pray that we may never be exposed to such a temptation."* (BOSC). In *The Blue Carbuncle*, which occurs during Christmas, the accused cries out to Holmes: *Oh, don't bring it into court! For Christ's sake, don't!"*

*Scandal in Bohemia and the Adler family:* ---- The story is set in 1888. It is pre-Dreyfus (1894) and pre-Theodore Herzl and the national cause of Zionism (1895 *et seq.*). Britain is overwhelmed with massive immigration of Jews from eastern Europe. They were besieged, poor, unskilled, and medieval in religious observance. At this time, between Aug. 31,1888 and Nov. 9, 1888, Jack the Ripper is at work; Jewish men are suspected (the "Juiwes", a vernacular spelling, appears in a graffiti accusation).

RABBI NATHAN ADLER

From 1844 to 1890, Rabbi Nathan Adler was chief rabbi of the Hebrew Congregation of Britain. The descriptive word is "Hebrew". He centralized Britain's synagogues into the United Hebrew Congregations of Britain. He began regular use of the title "rabbi" in England; prior to that time, "reverend" was equally applicable to Jewish men of religion. He was the first university-educated British Chief Rabbi as well as a Talmudic scholar. Where would Rabbi Akiva'smishnah --had it existed--have lain but in the Adler chambers? Nathan Adler standardized Hebrew education and corresponded with synagogues around the British empire. He warned rabbis in Poland and Russia of the conditions facing Jewish refugees in London's slums. His sermons referenced contemporary issues: Queen Victoria's births, Montefiore's travels to then-Palestine, the downtrodden Jews.

Rabbi Nathan made the news in the British papers and the *Jewish Chronicle*. He was contemporaneously described as the "highest religious authority not only of London Jews but of all Orthodox Jews throughout the United Kingdom and the Empire." Both Sir Moses Montefiore and Queen Victoria recognized his having served the rabbinate with honor and distinction. And this recognition of Rabbi Nathan wouldn't have been noted by Sherlock Holmes? When Moses Montefiore died in 1885, Rabbi Adler presided, as he had for Judith Montefiore some years prior. Cecil Roth wrote in retrospect that Rabbi Nathan had been "the father of the Anglo-Jewish pulpit." How would Holmes or Doyle not have been aware of this Rabbi Adler?

RABBI HERMANN ADLER

Or was the "Hebrew rabbi" Hermann Adler (son of Nathan) as Ms. Berman posited? He served officially from 1891 to 1911, though for some years prior, he had supplemented his father's duties as infirmities set in. Unlike his father, Hermann did not pursue his rabbinate entirely as a Talmudist. In fact, his PhD thesis was on a topic that might have piqued Holmes: "on Druidism." Rabbi Hermann also wrote *The Jews in England* (1899) among other publications on Anglo-Jewry. He was witty, urbane, and socially prominent among Jews and non-Jews. At a luncheon with British Catholic cardinal Herbert Vaughan, he was asked: "Now, Dr. Adler, when may I have the pleasure of helping you to some ham?" The rabbi responded: "At Your Eminence's wedding." In 1888, the *Jewish Standard* reported that Rabbi Hermann Adler led a discussion of Rabbi Akiva --but this was themishnaic scholar from 18th century Posen, not the classicist from the early part of the century. This Akiva would have interested the Anglo-Jewish community, composed as it was of so many eastern Europeans. This Rabbi Akiva could not have been the "Hebrew rabbi" of *Scandal* since he used a patronymic...Rabbi AkivaEiger...he would have been listed under "E".

The *Times* published a letter from Rabbi Hermann in which he responded to the accusations that Jews were suspects in the Jack the Ripper murders. One of the murders occurred near the High Holidays of Rosh Hashanah and Yom Kippur (the Day of Atonement). The idea that a Jew would transgress during these days of preparation and atonement was unlikely as many Jews were newly-arrived and tradition-bound.

However, if anyone promoted a reform movement, it would have been Rabbi Hermann *mishpocha* (family). Rabbi Hermann had even supported cremation. His daughter, Henrietta Adler, age 20 in 1888, was a formidable champion of women's rights. Like Irene Adler, she was possessed of both cleverness and "woman's wit." Unable to stand for election, she used the prestige of her name to rally Jewish support behind progressive candidates and ultimately became a London council member. We needn't look to N.Y.

Rabbi Samuel Adler and try to place him in this puzzle of who was the "Hebrew rabbi".

### *"Hebrew rabbi":*

Both words--"Hebrew" and "rabbi"-- were used because the gentile public would not necessarily have been familiar with "rabbi" standing alone. They had been alternatively cast as "reverends". References to educated or religious Jews were as Hebrews---a pious turn of phrase. The Adlers were rabbis of the United Hebrew Congregations of the British Empire. Jews were referred to as "Israelites" as had been Benjamin Disraeli, or "the brethren." In *Shoscombe Old Place*,Sir Robert is deeply in the hands of ....the Jews. Fear not, for Sir Robert holds off those...Jews. Jews were peddlers, brokers, travelers, money lenders and/or aliens. They were suspects in the Jack the Ripper murders. Hebrews, though antiquated, were respectable.

### *"It had to be You":*

Beyond peradventure, a British Adler was the considered Hebrew rabbi of *Scandal*...not one from ancient Palestine and certainly not a New Yorker.

The *Jewish Chronicle* wrote on July 21,1891 (*Scandal of Bohemia* publication: July 1891): Nathan Adler and Hermann Adler "gave their name to a regime, to an era... to the system of Rabbinate which had long come to be known as 'Adlerism', the keynote of which was the close consolidation of religious government and the concentration of ecclesiastical control... "

Perhaps Doyle had in mind a mingling of all these Adlers-- for there were yet more extraordinary and distinguished among them, and all during this same period. A brother to Hermann was Elkan Adler (1861–1946). He was an author, lawyer, historian, and collector of Jewish books and manuscripts. He worked for Moses Montefiore and thus travelled extensively to the Holy Land. Elkan was among the first to explore the documents stored in Cairo. From his 1895 visit there, he brought over 25,000 manuscript fragments back to England and built an enormous library of old Jewish documents.

It could not have been yet another brother, Marcus Adler, because he was not a rabbi. He was no less illustrious for he was an actuary, vice-president of the Institute of Actuaries, a founder of the Royal Statistical and London Mathematical Societies, and a publisher as well.

The Adler women weren't an afterthought--recall Henrietta, Rabbi Hermann's daughter. Rabbi Hermann also had a sister--Ida, born in 1860, and sandwiched between her accomplished brothers. She married diamond broker Magnus Schaap in 1881. As had Godfrey Norton and Irene Adler fled London after their wedding, so too did Ida and her husband, fleeing emblematically andanglicizing their last name to "Sharp."


_In Conclusion:_

In the context of the years 1888-1891, it is indisputable that one of the remarkable Adlers of London, or an aggregate, were the "Hebrew rabbi" of Holmes' scrapbook.

# The Trial of Mycroft Holmes

From details provided in *The Greek Interpreter* -- ο Έλληνας διερμηνέας (serialized in the Strand Magazine, 1893)

MYCROFT HOLMES' BACKGROUND

Mycroft Holmes is Sherlock's senior by seven years. He is reportedly fat and exceptionally brilliant. He seldom moves from his accustomed cycle: his rooms, his office in a government building, and the Diogenes Club where silence is obligatory. Mycroft is at the Club regularly from 4:45 p.m. to 7:40 p.m., sufficient time for a prodigious High Tea. He is lethargic. It's brother Sherlock who combines both brilliance and energy. Mycroft works for Her Majesty's government. In the Greek Interpreter, Holmes informs us, vaguely, that Mycroft "audits the books in some of the government departments."

In the Bruce Partington Plans, Watson learns that Mycroft has a position of importance and prestige: "occasionally he is the British government . . . the most indispensable man in the country. We will suppose that a minister needs information as to a point which involves the Navy, India, Canada and the bimetallic question; he could get his separate advices from various departments upon each, but only Mycroft can focus them all, and say offhand how each factor would affect the other."

Keep in mind Mycroft's expertise.
In the *Greek Interpreter*, we react with measured awe as the brothers, Sherlock and Mycroft, engage in the art of deduction as they develop the status of a man they observe walking outside the window.

Did Mycroft participate in any crimes in the Greek Interpreter?
Can he be held accountable for his conduct?

## THE STORY IN A NUTSHELL...the baklava:

Mycroft lives in the same building as does Mr. Melas, well-known Greek interpreter for foreign guests in London hotels. On a Monday evening, Melas is lured to an unknown destination by Harold Latimer, one of the kidnappers. There he is ordered to translate for an emaciated prisoner, whose face is covered with sticking-plaster (bandages) to make it difficult to recognize him. Their prisoner is Greek and doesn't speak English. Melas shows strength under pressure. Cleverly, he adds a question in Greek to those he is told to ask the prisoner, and is able to learn a few things. He is interrupted in the furtive translation by a tall, dark woman who enters and recognizes the prisoner as her brother Paul Kratides. She is Sophy Kratides, who apparently eloped with Latimer, which wasn't sufficient to turn over the family fortune to the kidnappers. Sophy seemed helpless but Kemp and Latimer would soon learn that a more apt description of Sophy would be "still waters run deep." The kidnappers threaten Melas with retaliation, pay him five sovereigns, take him by coach to an isolated heath outside London, and dump him there at midnight. In the dark, he meets up with a railway porter who tells him he has to walk but a mile to catch the last train for Victoria Station.

The next day, Tuesday, Melas goes to the police. They don't believe him. Though he's an educated Englishman, he has a foreign look to him..."Greek by extraction," says Sherlock Holmes. Melas then goes to Mycroft's rooms and asks him to lend assistance.

Later, Mycroft will tell Dr. Watson that he listened attentively to Melas, from whose account he made "some very pleasing speculations." He made an inquiry to the Greek Legation but they were noncommittal, perhaps otherwise engaged in that Mediterranean country's debt default and restructuring of 1893.

Mycroft then placed this ad in the daily papers:
"Anybody supplying any information to the whereabouts of a Greek gentleman named Paul Kratides, from Athens, who is unable to speak English, will be rewarded. A similar reward paid to anyone giving information about a Greek lady whose first name is Sophy.    X 2473."

The kidnappers were thus alerted to Melas' loose lips and would retaliate by re-kidnapping him.

J. Davenport answered the ad and informs Mycroft as to the location of the house where he saw Sophy and where Paul Kratides was being held. The kidnappers escape and take Sophy with them. They leave behind their bound victims. Paul Kratides is dead, and Melas is almost dead from suffocation in a shut room with a lit charcoal brazier that was generating noxious fumes--in the manner of an 1893 London factory in smoky and polluting production.

Several months later, the Times from Budapest reports that two Englishmen, traveling with a Greek lady, had argued, fought, and stabbed one another fatally.   Holmes believed Sophy Kratides murdered them and got her revenge.

LIKELY CRIMINAL CHARGES…
1. attempted murder-- the bludgeoning and charcoaling of the Greek interpreter, Mr. Melas, who survived.
2. the murder of Paul Kratides.  The conspirators, Kemp and Latimer, kidnapped Mr. Melas in order to communicate with Paul, who then died from starvation and charcoal smoke.

3. The re-Kidnapping: Melas was kidnapped twice; the re-kidnapping occurred after the kidnappers learned he had talked because Mycroft placed the ad in the daily papers.
4. Assault and battery: of Melas.

WOULD THE GOVERNMENT BEAR A RESPONSIBILITY FOR MYCROFT'S CONDUCT?

WHAT WAS MYCROFT'S DUTY, WHETHER IN AN INDIVIDUAL CAPACITY OR AS AGENT FOR HER MAJESTY'S GOVERNMENT?

The Kratides and Melas case were conceivably outside the scope of Mycroft's employment, so one cannot presume to draw in the Government as co- defendant (in any case, the Government generally holds immunity from lawsuits such as these). On the other hand, why did the usually indolent Mycroft accompany Sherlock and Dr. Watson to the scene unless he was necessary to the criminal investigation, perhaps for his diplomatic and government connections?
Once he agreed to become involved, what then was required of Mycroft in duty and performance? Could he be charged for being less electric in results? What had Melas expected of Mycroft?

Melas was possibly anticipating the assistance of Mycroft's brother, the Great Detective. He must have trusted Mycroft. Mycroft made no unlawful misrepresentations about himself or his expertise. He even admitted to Watson that he wasn't particularly competent in this investigation: "Sherlock has all the energy of the family," said Mycroft, turning to me. "Well, you take the case up by all means, and let me know if you do any good."

Did it matter whether or not Mycroft was paid by Mr. Melas? No. A volunteer may be held responsible just as would a good samaritan on the roadside.

## WILL THE CROWN (REGINA) PREVAIL IN A PROSECUTION OF MYCROFT?

It is doubtful that Mycroft could be charged with the intentional murder of Paul Kratides or the attempted murder of Mr. Melas. There was no orchestration on his part, no intent, and he wasn't present. The defense would more than likely overcome the prosecution's case and show that the murder and attempted murder were preconceived by Kemp and Latimer in their attempt to wrest financial control over the Kratides fortune.

A trickier charge to overcome would be criminal negligence, which is a little criminal a little civil...and not as difficult a burden for the prosecution. Recall that the plaintiffs in OJ's civil trial, and in Robert Blake's civil trial, won with a lesser burden of proof.

With negligence, it's not "beyond a reasonable doubt. " Legal terminology for proof of liability can be a dense thicket. Suffice it to summarize that

---Causation in negligence can be explained as "but for" Mycroft's advertisement, Paul Kratides would not have died, Melas would not have been re-kidnapped, Melas would not have been injured, and Sophy would not have been hauled off to parts unknown by the kidnappers. Did Mycroft's ad lead to the criminal acts?

---The facts must be such that there is an unbroken chain of causation from Mycroft to advertisement to the wrongful acts.

---Should Mycroft, as a reasonable, astute man, been able to foresee the outcome of his ad?

---Was the ad and its disclosures mean-spirited?

---Was Mycroft wilful in putting Melas, Paul, and Sophy at risk?

---Could an advertisement result in murder? (as has occurred with the modern Craigslist? No. Today's ads have directly involved the actual parties and victims, and not third parties.)

Rest easy!

The general rule: publication of an ad is not an extreme and outrageous act. Here, there was no puffery, no hyperbole, no inflated facts, no emotional rendering.


THE TRIAL circa 1893

All the jurors would have been men. The pubs outside the Old Bailey would be filled with carousers and court watchers. St. Sepulchre church was nearby and available for a whispered prayer for or from an accused. Mycroft would have been led into the Old Bailey courthouse through a tunnel underneath from Newgate Prison.

What were the conditions at Newgate? Oscar Wilde was held there for his 1895 trial on sodomy---the love that dared not speak its name--until his bail was posted. There was no ventilation. There were no toilets, and inmates used a tin can in the cell to which they were confined all day. There were no mattresses; Oscar Wilde slept on a board. They were made to walk six miles in a circle, daily. Utter silence was imposed at all times. They were fed porridge and cocoa.

Why the gift of cocoa? Cadbury had made its prosperous industrial chocolate name in England, and, having been established and operated by the heretofore persecuted Quakers, donated regularly to poor houses, prisons, the John Howard Society and orphans' homes.

In the courtroom, spectator seats in an important trial would have included London's Lord Mayor, aldermen, clerks and important members of the clergy, with a few remaining for relatives, interested parties, and the public.

The defendant would take a seat on the dock, a raised platform, and would stand when requested. Mycroft, standing in the dock with his prison warden, had the right not to testify… to prevent self-incrimination. Mycroft would know from the Diogenes Club that "silence is golden." Oscar Wilde did not avail himself of the privilege in the first of his trials and was ravaged on cross-examination by Sir Edward Carson.

THE JUDGE: The Lord Chief Justice sat on a raised, crimson-cushioned bench. He wore crimson red for ceremonial occasions and a full wig, but presiding in a run-of-the-mill criminal case, he would wear a less ostentatious black damask gown daubed with gold lace and his short wig.

THE WITNESSES
Who would testify in the Mycroft Holmes trial?

The landlady at the Mycroft and Melas premises.
Mr. Melas, Mr. J. Davenport, Sherlock Holmes, Dr. Watson
Inspector Gregson;
The police constable with whom Melas spoke
The chemist who sold sticking plaster to the giggling gentleman

Staff from the hotel where Melas got the referral
The railway porter at Wandsworth Commons where Melas was dropped off

Both prosecution and defense can call these witnesses for their separate purposes.
Will these witnesses be enough for either side to prove their case?

CASE/ARGUMENT FOR THE CROWN:
The prosecutor opens the case. Both he and defense counsel wear silk black gowns. Traditionally, the prosecutor cannot appeal to emotion though heady reference to the classics muddied the rule. In Oscar Wilde's criminal trial, he recounted that the prosecutor's argument was an "appalling denunciation [of me]--like something out of Tacitus, like a passage in Dante, like one of Savonarola's indictments of the Popes of Rome."

The prosecutor lays out facts. He would seek to deflate the honor and integrity of Mycroft Holmes. He would manipulate the strengths of Mycroft's career, as well as that of his brother, to show that Mycroft possessed great sense, competence, and resources, and for which reason, the prosecution would urge, Mycroft's defense of stupidity, or, in the alternative, "no harm done" or "no duty owed" should be abjured by the jurors, and that common sense should prevail.

The Crown would show that as a government agent, long in her Majesty's service, Mycroft had the training and opportunity to identify and apprehend criminals. Instead, Mycroft found this case a bit of a lark during the time that two people were held against their will by two dangerous men.

He saw his brother and Watson over a day and a half after Mr. Melas had stopped by his rooms to request assistance. Mycroft hadn't asked Holmes and Watson to stop by; nor did he inquire of them. After placing the ad, he willfully abandoned Mr. Melas. He retreated to the Diogenes Club. Sherlock and Dr. Watson happened to come to see him. Can we reasonably infer that the police informed THEM about the case which they had first heard from Mr. Melas?

It was a Wednesday evening by the time of the Holmes' brothers and Dr. Watson's meeting. Mycroft mentioned the case to them quite casually. Yet, Melas had had his first encounter with Kemp and Latimer on Monday evening. Mycroft placed the ad by Tuesday. The ad was simply too explicit when he should have withheld some information in the interest of safety. His brother wouldn't have revealed his hand.

Mycroft Holmes, from all the aforementioned facts, failed to act reasonably under the circumstances. What should he have done? He should have gone to the police and caused a warrant to be issued. He had the authority to demand that the police respond. Mycroft admitted that he failed to go to the police. The jury should give ample weight to the admission of the amply endowed Defendant that he was guilty of inaction and incompetence.

Mr. Melas was the hero in this case...he was treated shabbily, even criminally, by Mycroft Holmes. Mr. Melas' quick mind must be commended. When he was first in that room with Paul Kratides, even after being threatened by Kemp and Latimer, he kept his wits about him and obtained vital information from Paul.

The jurors may choose to find Mycroft liable on the lesser offense. He should not be absolved and let off scot free. His self-professed stupidity in placing the ad was wanton and criminal because he put human beings in harm's way.

AN ALTERNATIVE FOR THE PROSECUTION:
Mycroft was stalling after Melas came to see him. But why and for what reason? Perhaps Mr. Melas was not such an innocent, and perhaps the police, when they spoke with Mr. Melas, recognized this, or knew of his unsavory employment. Mycroft and Melas may have been working together. Mr. Melas' career was that of interpreter for foreigners staying in London hotels, and, coincidentally, he and an agent of the Crown, Mycroft Holmes, resided in the same building. They were discussing the Kratides case as allies.

The prosecution cannot be in the business of coincidences, admittedly, yet how else does one explain Kemp and Latimer's connection to Melas and the Northumberland Avenue hotel staff? Neither of them were "wealthy Orientals." Mycroft Holmes must have made them aware of Melas' Greek facility.

Melas and Mycroft were complicit in the placement of the ad (In such an instance, the prosecution would do well to make unavailable the witness Melas, and situate him elsewhere on the Continent.). On the other hand, Mycroft knew to dispose of Melas, a witness to the kidnapping fiasco. With the placement of the ad, Kemp and Latimer had time to dispose of Paul Kratides and whoever else. The ad was a signal: "The plan is known. Your covers are blown. Charcoal for 2 and flight with number 3." Mycroft's ad was THE fatal cause of Paul's death. He knew he had been starved and was in perilously weak condition. As Mycroft stalled and engaged in conversation with his brother and Dr. Watson, Kemp and Latimer's charcoal fire was smoking.

## MYCROFT HOLMES' DEFENSE
Defense lawyers were rarely used until the late 19th century. Even then, few defendants were able to afford a lawyer unless the Crown appointed one, as it would in cases of murder.

Mycroft's defense would argue that, he being of aristocratic lineage, the idea that he was allied with criminal sorts was laughable were not the Defendant on trial for his life and his reputation.

Mycroft's career with British intelligence was long and formidable. He kept foreign enemies at bay and the British Isles safe. In the British Secret Service, the "M" in MI 5 and MI 6 (domestic and foreign intelligence) may in fact be short for "Mycroft." He was a mathematical genius with an extraordinary faculty for figures…the Alan Turing of the 19th century.

His personal characteristics reveal a predictable and enviable circumspection. He had fixed, regular, and dependable habits without a scintilla of deviation such as this murderous foray for financial gain.

And Melas? The jury must be persuaded that he simply brought the circumstances upon himself, without any assistance from Mycroft Holmes. He got his business contacts, distastefully, from hotel staff. He was a risk-taker. He was rather "gleeful," as Dr. Watson described him, and who also said Melas had eyes "sparkling with pleasure." The defense would submit that Melas' glee arose from his undue attraction to risky behavior.

Melas told Mycroft that he was impressed with Latimer being "fashionably dressed." Melas, a professional, thought it reasonable to leave his house at 7:15 at night, with a perfect stranger, because his clothing was fashionable, to go to an undisclosed location.

He took on unknown clients in unfamiliar locales. All for the sake of a fee. He wasn't regularly employed. How on earth did he afford his membership at the Diogenes Gentlemen's Club or his rooms in the Pall Mall? Melas placed himself in risky circumstances, whatever the consequences, in search of a fee.

The police didn't believe Melas...they didn't find him credible...Why should the jurors find him believable or the prosecutor's version of Melas' nobility.

And the ad: Sherlock Holmes himself said that agony columns "are always instructive" and "Surely the most valuable hunting ground that ever was given..." (Red Circle). Mycroft selflessly offered a reward...to save Paul and Sophy...in an advertisement, a tactic learned from the Great Detective. There was nothing irresponsible or unprofessional about the use of personal advertisements in the course of Mycroft's criminal investigation...not criminal conduct. It may arguably have been a blunder, but it wasn't a criminal act. As soon as there was an answer to the ad from J. Davenport, Mycroft was roused to immediate action and a trip to Lower Brixton to interview him.

Looking back at the scene of the crime: In what condition did Melas find Paul Kratides when he first arrived? At death's door and deadly pale. Was this attributable to Mycroft? Certainly not. Those two, Kemp and Latimer, intended Paul Kratides' death at the outset. Whether he signed or not, Paul was not going to leave alive. No advertisement was responsible for Paul's kidnap, assault, battery and death. It began three full weeks' prior.

There is worse yet about Melas. Kemp was elderly, giggly, and somewhat mad. He appeared to have a nervous malady akin to St. Vitus' Dance. Melas was left alone in a room with the unsteady Kemp. What effort did he make to save Paul? None. He groveled and bowed. He told Mycroft that he feared the old man's EYES. This was his reaction while Paul Kratides was being starved to death. He also congratulated himself on his conduct. He told Mycroft it was "fortunate" that he himself took no steps. Was he paid by the kidnappers? Yes. Kemp gave him five sovereigns, and Melas did not refuse the fee.

"It's every man's business to see justice done." Sherlock Holmes, *The Crooked Man.*

"Watson, you are a British jury, and I never met a man who was more eminently fitted to represent one." Sherlock Holmes, *Abbey Grange.*

WHAT SHOULD BE THE VERDICT OF THE GENTLEMEN AND GENTLEWOMEN OF THE JURY IN THE TRIAL OF MYCROFT HOLMES?

# Also from MX Publishing

MX Publishing is the world's largest specialist Sherlock Holmes publisher, with over a hundred titles and fifty authors creating the latest in Sherlock Holmes fiction and non-fiction.

From traditional short stories and novels to travel guides and quiz books, MX Publishing cater for all Holmes fans.

The collection includes leading titles such as *Benedict Cumberbatch In Transition* and *The Norwood Author* which won the 2011 Howlett Award (Sherlock Holmes Book of the Year).

MX Publishing also has one of the largest communities of Holmes fans on Facebook with regular contributions from dozens of authors.

www.mxpublishing.com

# Also from MX Publishing

Our bestselling books are our short story collections;

'Lost Stories of Sherlock Holmes' , 'The Outstanding
Mysteries of Sherlock Holmes', The Papers of Sherlock
Holmes Volume 1 and 2, 'Untold Adventures of Sherlock
Holmes' (and the sequel 'Studies in Legacy) and 'Sherlock
Holmes in Pursuit', 'The Cotswold Werewolf and Other
Stories of Sherlock Holmes' – and many more……

www.mxpublishing.com

# Also from MX Publishing

"Phil Growick's, 'The Secret Journal of Dr Watson', is an adventure which takes place in the latter part of Holmes and Watson's lives. They are entrusted by HM Government (although not officially) and the King no less to undertake a rescue mission to save the Romanovs, Russia's Royal family from a grisly end at the hand of the Bolsheviks. There is a wealth of detail in the story but not so much as would detract us from the enjoyment of the story. Espionage, counter-espionage, the ace of spies himself, double-agents, double-crossers...all these flit across the pages in a realistic and exciting way. All the characters are extremely well-drawn and Mr Growick, most importantly, does not falter with a very good ear for Holmesian dialogue indeed. Highly recommended. A five-star effort."
**The Baker Street Society**

www.mxpublishing.com

# Also from MX Publishing

## The Missing Authors Series

Sherlock Holmes and The Adventure of The Grinning Cat
Sherlock Holmes and The Nautilus Adventure
Sherlock Holmes and The Round Table Adventure

"Joseph Svec, III is brilliant in entwining two endearing and enduring classics of literature, blending the factual with the fantastical; the playful with the pensive; and the mischievous with the mysterious. We shall, all of us young and old, benefit with a cup of tea, a tranquil afternoon, and a copy of Sherlock Holmes, The Adventure of the Grinning Cat."
**Amador County Holmes Hounds Sherlockian Society**

www.mxpublishing.com

# Also from MX Publishing

## The American Literati Series

The Final Page of Baker Street
The Baron of Brede Place
Seventeen Minutes To Baker Street

"The really amazing thing about this book is the author's ability to call up the 'essence' of both the Baker Street 'digs' of Holmes and Watson as well as that of the 'mean streets' of Marlowe's Los Angeles. Although none of the action takes place in either place, Holmes and Watson share a sense of camaraderie and self-confidence in facing threats and problems that also pervades many of the later tales in the Canon. Following their conversations and banter is a return to Edwardian England and its certainties and hope for the future. This is definitely the world before The Great War."
**Philip K Jones**

www.mxpublishing.com

# Also from MX Publishing

## The Detective and The Woman Series

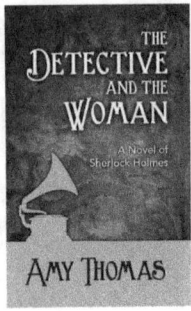 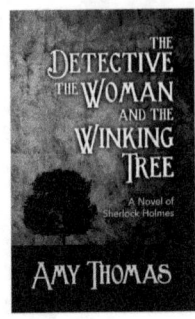 

The Detective and The Woman
The Detective, The Woman and The Winking Tree
The Detective, The Woman and The Silent Hive

"The book is entertaining, puzzling and a lot of fun. I believe the author has hit on the only type of long-term relationship possible for Sherlock Holmes and Irene Adler. The details of the narrative only add force to the romantic defects we expect in both of them and their growth and development are truly marvelous to watch. This is not a love story. Instead, it is a coming-of-age tale starring two of our favorite characters."
**Philip K Jones**

www.mxpublishing.com

# Also from MX Publishing

## The Sherlock Holmes and Enoch Hale Series

The Amateur Executioner
The Poisoned Penman
The Egyptian Curse

"The Amateur Executioner: Enoch Hale Meets Sherlock Holmes", the first collaboration between Dan Andriacco and Kieran McMullen, concerns the possibility of a Fenian attack in London. Hale, a native Bostonian, is a reporter for London's Central News Syndicate - where, in 1920, Horace Harker is still a familiar figure, though far from revered. "The Amateur Executioner" takes us into an ambiguous and murky world where right and wrong aren't always distinguishable. I look forward to reading more about Enoch Hale."
**Sherlock Holmes Society of London**